About the Author

Helen lives with her husband, Chris, daughter, Isla, and Sonny the fluffy ragdoll cat. She studied at Liverpool John Moores University where she gained a degree in Media & Cultural Studies and Screen studies (BA Hons) and went on to spend time working as part of the team producing digital content for popular Channel 4 programme Hollyoaks. After further studies at the University of Chester, Helen also qualified as a Primary School teacher. Helen now works as an Executive Assistant and writes in her spare time. She enjoys reading, arts and crafts and spending time with family and friends.

Mrs Muddle

Mrs Muddle

Written by Helen E Jones
Illustrations by Helen Highton Gottberg

www.olympiapublishers.com
OLYMPIA PAPERBACK EDITION

A CIP catalogue record for this title is available from the British Library.

ISBN: 978-1-78830-729-1
First Published in 2020

Olympia Publishers
Tallis House
2 Tallis Street
London
EC4Y 0AB

Printed in Great Britain

Dedication

For my beautiful daughter Isla.
May you always have the courage and strength to be yourself and to know your worth.

Mrs Muddle was a very nice lady,
She smiled at everyone she met.
One day a little mouse crept into her house
So she kept him as her pet!

Mrs Muddle and the mouse became the best of friends
They would dance and sing all day
They would swim in the lake, even bake a cake
And laugh all their troubles away

Mrs Muddle was five foot tall
And her face was full of cheer.
She loved to sing loudly and sang her songs proudly
Not worrying about who may hear.

Mrs Muddle wasn't like other people,
She chose to do things her own way.
She didn't feel shy if people asked, "why"
Or worry about what they might say.

On a rainy day you'd often see
Dear old Mrs Muddle
Dash out of her house with her little pet mouse
And together they'd splash in a puddle.

Their wellies would be soaking wet
They'd squidge and squelch in the sludge.
Then splish and splash, through the rain they'd dash
And back home to dry off they'd trudge

Mrs Muddle's favourite food
was chicken in custard and jam.
She ate chocolate covered cheese with fish fingers and peas
And had ice cream scoops on her ham.

She always liked to read her books
Starting from the very last chapter
Because that way, you see, she'd make sure there would be
A happily ever after.

Mrs Muddle's trousers were too short for her legs
And her hat was too big for her head.
She wore sandals in the snow and her clothes didn't go
And she wore a woolly hat to bed.

She dyed her hair green every Sunday,
Then on a Tuesday she'd dye it bright red.
By Thursday she'd think that she wished it was pink,
So she'd wear a pink wig on her head.

Mrs Muddle rode a rusty, brown bike
with a basket on the front for her mouse.
With the wind in her hair, she had not a care
As she peddled through the lanes by her house.

The lambs would see her riding along
And 'baaa baaa' they would bleet.
The lambs were delighted and oh so excited
When she gave them some corn as a treat.

Ali and Jessica lived down the lane
And they saw Mrs Muddle each day.
They wanted to find out, without any doubt,
Why she did things in a different way.

So one hot summer's evening
when they saw her skipping down the street
They called out her name and over she came
with her wellington boots on her feet!

"We wondered why you're so different..." Ali asked,
"...to other people we see?"
She thought for a while and said with a smile,
"Well, my dear, I'm just being me!

"I don't want to be like everyone else,
I live my life how I like.
s more fun, you see, when I'm just being me
And riding my rusty, brown bike.

"I don't want to follow the crowd
And drive a shiny new car,
So children be proud and shout it out loud
Be free to be just who you are!"

Later that night when the children were home
They discussed what Mrs Muddle had said.
They started to see how fun it could be
To do things their own way instead.

But Ali worried what other boys would think
If his hair wasn't cut the same as theirs.
What if the boys made fun of his toys?
Or the type of clothes he wears?

Jessica worried what other girls would say
If she didn't wear a skirt or play house.
She'd rather wear dungarees and have fun climbing trees,
But then along came Mrs Muddle's mouse...

He squeaked, "Why do you both look so worried?
It would be boring if we were all the same!
So go and be free, be who you should be!
If you didn't it would be such a shame!"

So when they got dressed the next morning
Jessica wore a cape, not a dress.
Ali wore jeans that were stained with baked beans
As he no longer had to impress.

A little while later their mum came and asked them
what they would like for their lunch.
They chose egg and sardines with big tangerines
And a mango and spinach punch.

Their mum looked puzzled as she watched them eat
And Dolly, the dog, was bemused.
They usually ate beans, never sardines...
Dolly was quite confused.

That afternoon when Jessica's friend came round
They didn't do what they'd always done.
They didn't play dolls... instead they played trolls
And together they had so much fun!

Ali went to his friend's house
And showed him his brand new hair.
His friend was impressed and loved how he dressed
Ali felt so happy being there!

That evening whilst playing with their favourite toys
In their little red wendy house.
Out of the corner of her eye, Jessica did spy
Mrs Muddle's little pet mouse.

"You took Mrs Muddle's advice!" the mouse squeaked,
"You're smiling and happy, you see?!
You're being true to the real you
And that's the best way to be!"

Now the children were happy just being themselves
And not having to follow the crowd.
They were still exceptional, irreplaceable, special
And the mouse felt so very proud.